Happy Birthday Maddy!

Love,
Grammy & Pepere'

Hi. I'm Numbear!

The number 2 is **TREMENDOUS**,
let me tell you why...

A **giraffe** only needs 2 hours of sleep each night.

Tarantulas can live without food for 2 years.

The 2nd planet in the solar system is **Venus**, named after the Roman goddess of love and beauty.

Mercury

Venus

Earth

Eris

Pluto

Mars

Jupiter

Saturn

Uranus

Neptune

In the 2 years since you were born ...
The **Earth** has travelled around the Sun twice.
The **Moon** has gone around Earth about 26 times.
Our **World** has turned 730 times (once every day).

In your **2 years** you have spent
over one year asleep.

Your **heart** has beaten about 70 million times.

Hair can grow 12cm **every year** and fingernails can grow 0.1mm a day.

So if you didn't cut them they would

look like this when you're a grown up!

So you see, 2 really is **awesome!**

2 as a word

TWO

2 on a card

2 on a dice

2 o'clock

2 in other languages

French - 'deux'
Spanish - 'dos'
German - 'zwei'
Russian - 'dva'
Latin - 'duo'

The 2nd month of the year

2 in Roman numerals

January	February	March	April
May	June	July	August
September	October	November	December

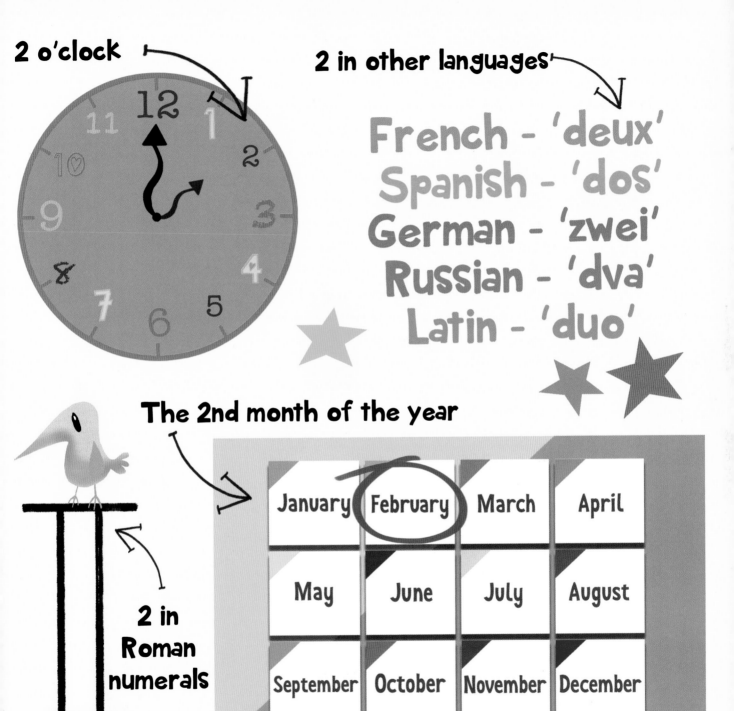

But the
GREATEST
thing about the
number 2 is . . .

Now You Are Two first published by **FORGET ME NOT BOOKS**, an imprint of **FROM YOU TO ME LTD,** September2020

FROM YOU TO ME, Waterhouse, Waterhouse Lane, Monkton Combe, Bath, BA2 7JA, UK

FORGET® me NOT BOOKS

For a full range of all our titles where journals & books can also be personalised, please visit

WWW.FROMYOUTOME.COM

Each child is unique so all data used is averaged. Sleep information is based on UK NHS sleep requirement data.

1 3 5 7 9 11 13 15 14 12 10 8 6 4 2

Printed and bound in China. This paper is manufactured from pulp sourced from forests that are legally and sustainably managed.

Written and illustrated by Lucy Tapper & Steve Wilson fromlucy.com

ISBN 978-1-907860-68-3

Available Titles: Now You Are 1, 2, 3, 4, 5, 6